One day, a small mouse was born on the outskirts of a great city.
AF480923

He didn't think like the other mice, and although he loved his family, he never quite felt at home.

What are they doing in there?
He always wanted to learn more about people and the world.

The mouse wanted so badly to understand the world that he decided to go against everything his family had told him about people.

He told the people about his life on the outskirts of the city and how he always wanted to learn about the world.

Each night, Charlie would visit his new friends and they would stay up talking and teaching him all about the world and life in the city.

As time went on, Charlie's curiosity grew and he found himself wondering more and more about the differences between people and other animals like himself.
I don't think anyone really knows.
It's up to each person to decide that for themselves.
What does it mean to be a human?
To have fun!

Every person that Charlie asked gave him a different answer.
To love God and each other with all your heart.

And although each answer seemed to be true in some way, none of them ever seemed to fully answer his question.

To suffer.
One day, Charlie got an answer that he had never considered.

That night, Charlie didn't go back to his friend's apartment. He couldn't get himself to stop thinking about what the old man had said "to suffer".
What did he mean?

Charlie decided that if he wanted to figure out what the old man meant, he would have to see and experience more of the world. He needed to find people and places that would teach him what it means to suffer.

Charlie traveled the world with his question in mind and saw many different types of people and ways to live.

He saw suffering of all
kinds and learned to know
the many different types.

Everywhere Charlie went, there were people suffering in different ways but he still couldn't understand what the old man had meant.

Charlie missed his friends and his family and eventually decided to go back to his home even though he never found the answer he was looking for.

On his way home, two people stopped him to ask if he would be able to help them harvest their crops.

Charlie had learned to
work hard from his travels
and it made him happy to
be able to help these people.

As the days passed and the harvest continued, Charlie found himself to be more and more happy in knowing that he was able to help his new friends. And when the family asked Charlie to stay through the winter, he felt at home for the first time in his short life.

One day, his friend cried out in the field and Charlie rushed to see if they were okay.

When he got there, Charlie saw the snake coiled up and ready to strike. Without thinking, Charlie jumped at the snake and scratched with all his might.

The snake slithered away in fear but not before sinking its venomous fangs into the little mouse. The family was horrified and didn't know how to help as Charlie looked up at them with a fading smile. In these last moments, he finally understood what the old man had told him so long ago, and with his final breath he said.

The
End

Scan the code below to explore other books by Alexander Pedersen

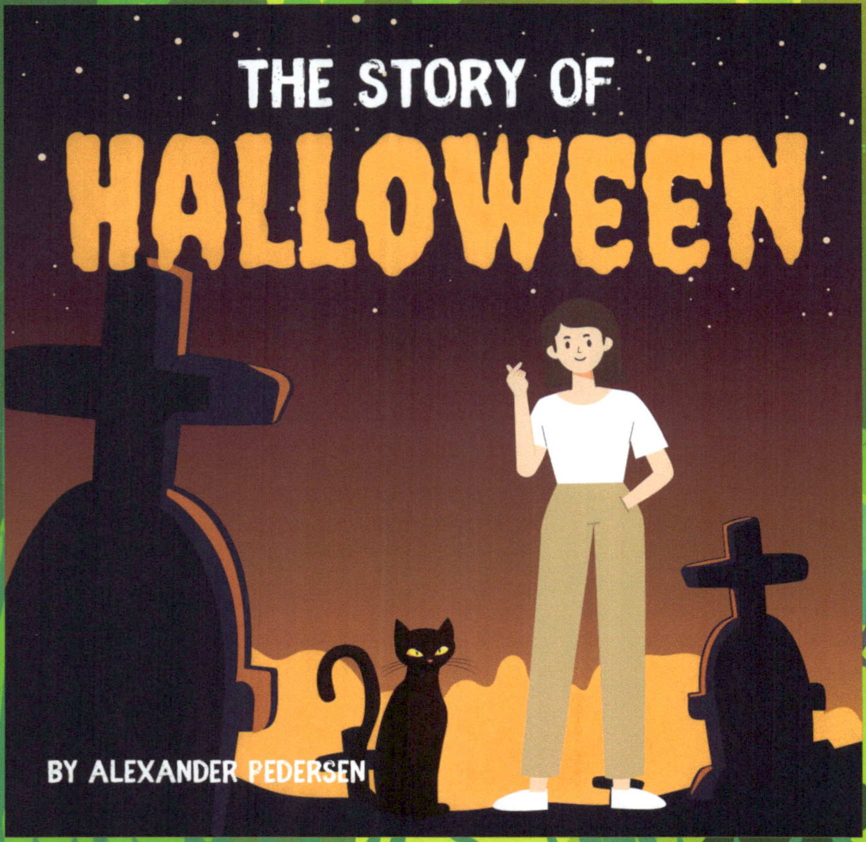

9 798778 561748